A Light in the Shadow

Written by Kaitlyn Brianna Guttridge

Illustrated by Joseph Forkan

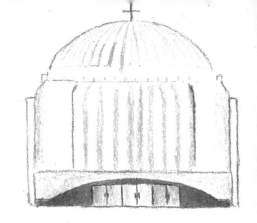

Dedication:
In honor of the brave men and women who lost their lives on 9/11.

To my family. For always supporting me, inspiring me, and allowing me to pursue my dreams, no matter how big.

To St. Nicholas Greek Orthodox Church and its parish. My hope is to bring to light and recognize the importance of the church's history and its bright place in the future.

~ Kaitlyn Guttridge

To those who lost their lives or loved ones on 9/11

To my family, friends, and art teachers, who have always encouraged me to pursue art.

~ Joseph Forkan

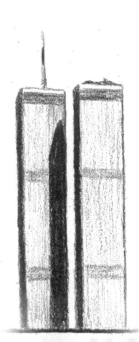

A Light in the Shadow

Written by Kaitlyn Brianna Guttridge

Illustrated by Joseph Forkan

Hi, my name is Anastasia, my friends call me Tessie. I am a beautiful white candle from Greece. I am almost one hundred years old. That is a long time to live. I have seen and heard many interesting things. This is the story of one of the most amazing things that could happen in a candle's lifetime. Before I get ahead of myself, let me start from the beginning.

In 1919, my family, friends, and I were placed
in a box in a factory in Greece,

and brought from Greece to live in a new land called America,
with a group of five families in New York City.

These families took us to a building at 155 Cedar Street, New York, NY. The families said that this building would be called St. Nicholas Greek Orthodox Church.

They started to take us out of the box and light us one-by-one. Being at the bottom of the box, I was able to hear what all of my family and friends were seeing and hearing while lit in the church over the years.

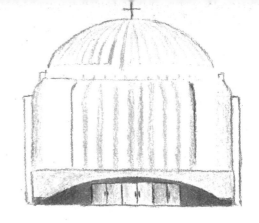

My cousin Thalia was the first to be lit, and she said that the church didn't look like much. "If you ask me," she said, "It looks like a place people once lived or ate in." "It is very small," she said, "yet so many people come to visit." "Tessie, all types of people are visiting this small church, from sailors to men working on Wall Street," said Thalia.

In 1922 the church officially opened its doors with
an exciting and wonderful celebration.

8

I liked it in the small church. After a while, I understood why those five families were so excited for their dream to become a reality!

Over the years, my family and I were able to watch and
listen to couples, both young and old, get married, see
babies get baptized by being dunked in water, watch many
Christmas pageants, and hear the most beautiful music.

On April 4, 1973, a young man came into the church, and my sister, Kasandra, overheard him talking to his brother. She told me that they were talking about these amazing buildings that had just been built right behind the church. Kasandra said the young man called them "The Twin Towers".

From what I have heard from my family over the years, these towers were really tall and beautiful. So tall, in fact, that the tiny Church of St. Nicholas sat in its shadow throughout the day.

Once, my friend Evelyn, said she
saw an elderly woman come into
the church with her daughter.
The old woman told her
daughter that the image
of the Twin Towers
behind St. Nicholas
was a beautiful sight
to behold, that even
though the church
stood in the
tower's shadow,
the church was a
bright light.

When Evelyn heard this, her flame grew taller with delight, while
I beamed, from the candle box, full of pride for my little church.

In 2000, my little church was filled with so many people, I could hear them all, even though the candle box was closed. Now, it was many more than five families who came to visit and sit in the church, and light candles; it was nearly seventy families!

Other people would come and visit too. Men and women in suits and business clothes, speaking all different languages, policemen and women on their lunch breaks, firemen after their shifts, as well as, women and children who stopped in on their way to Battery Park.

17

On September 11, 2001, as my brother Peter was lit by the window, he said to me, "It is a beautiful, clear, blue Tuesday outside. Summer's heat is not entirely gone yet. Boy, I wish you could see this Tessie."

Early in the morning, when all the people in business suits rushed to work, I heard a loud 'BOOM' above the church roof. It was so loud, that it knocked the lid right off of the candle box where I was kept. Now I could hear everything that was going on in and around the church.

It seemed like no one had known what happened and people sounded confused. Less than 20 minutes later, I heard another 'BOOM'. "What is going on," I asked Peter? "I don't know Tessie, people are running outside toward the back of the church. Something must have happened with the Twin Towers," Peter said.

From inside my opened candle box, I could hear people on the street and they sounded scared. I could hear people crying and anxiously asking questions that I could not hear the answers to.

I could hear the sirens of police cars, fire trucks, and ambulances rushing down the street. There were people trying to help others who were injured or who needed help. "There sure are a lot of policemen and firefighters out here Tessie," Peter said. "I hope everyone is alright," I said, as feelings of worry and sadness filled my mind.

Out of nowhere, at ten in the morning, my church started to shake and all I could hear was a loud rumble. I was so scared that I closed my eyes tight and hoped whatever was happening would be over soon.

All of the sudden I was knocked out of my box
and I fell onto the cold church floor.

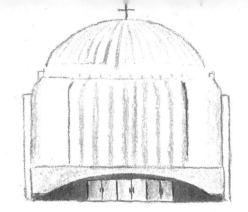

When I opened my eyes, I was in the dark, cold and scared.
I could hear loud machines and people; firefighters, police,
priests, and volunteers, digging through the rubble above me.

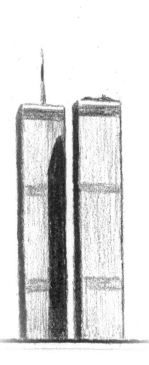

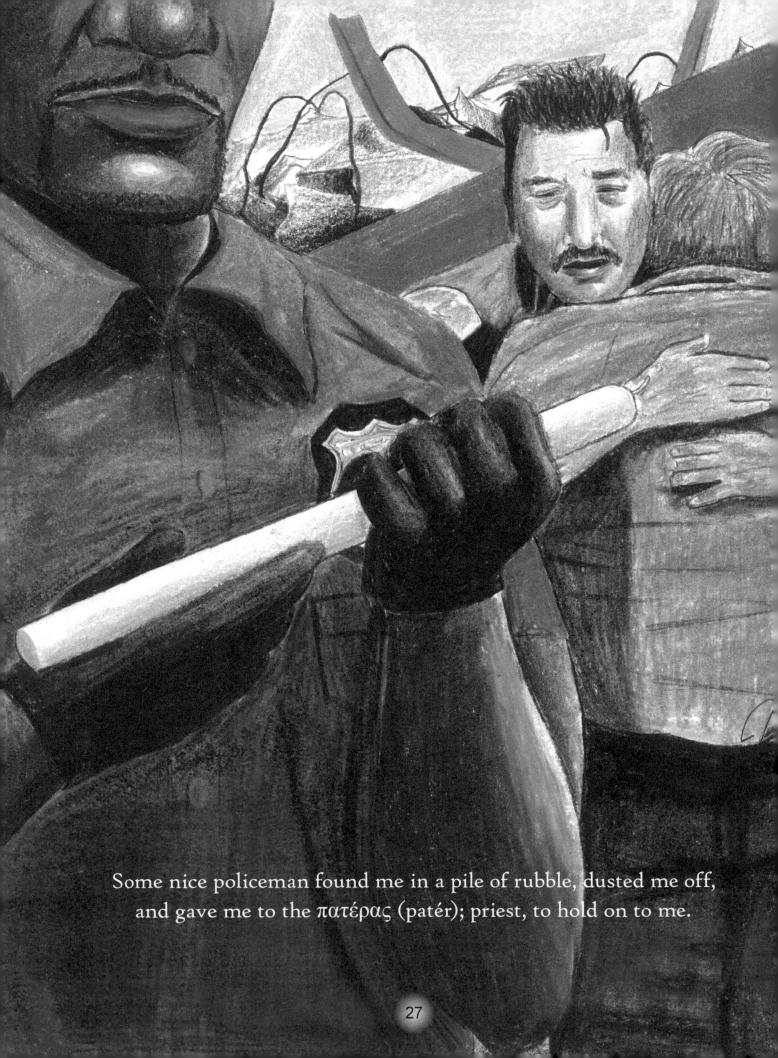

Some nice policeman found me in a pile of rubble, dusted me off, and gave me to the πατέρας (patér); priest, to hold on to me.

September 11, 2001 was the last time I was in my church. After being found in the rubble, I was placed in a box at the Archdiocese of New York, waiting for my church, my home, my St. Nicholas, to be rebuilt.

Fifteen years later, from the glass case where I now sit, I can hear people talking and they sound certain that St. Nicholas will be rebuilt. Listening to their conversations gives me hope for the future of St. Nicholas.

I am excited and overjoyed to
hear that we have broken ground.
This is the first step to building
the new St. Nicholas church.

Now, I hear from people's conversations that it won't be five families, it won't be seventy families, but it will be hundreds of families from all over the world that will light candles like me, and come visit my new St. Nicholas.

This new St. Nicholas will be three stories tall and will welcome everyone of all faiths and walks of life. This new St. Nicholas is going to be called a National Shrine.

People say that St. Nicholas'
Church and I are both the
light in the shadow, and I
can't wait to be placed in
my new home at 130 Liberty
Street, New York, New
York, and see all the new
candles shining bright.

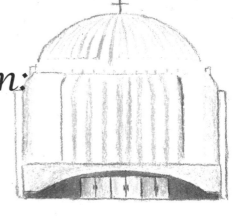

Anastasia's Album:

Before it was a church, the original building was used as a private home and then as a restaurant. After five Greek immigrant families bought the restaurant, it was changed into a church.

The original St. Nicholas Church was built long before the World Trade Center Twin Towers. After the towers were built, the small church stood in the incredibly large shadow of the two towers.

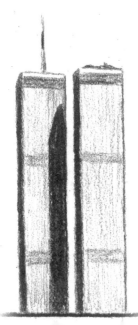

The original St. Nicholas was very small, it was only three floors.

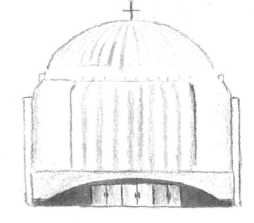

St. Nicholas was about eight pews long and two pews wide.

By September of 2001 the congregation was over 70 families large.

On September 11, 2001, terrorists hijacked two planes and crashed the planes into the World Trade Center Towers. This was not the only attack that day, terrorists also hijacked two other planes, one crashed into the Pentagon, while the last plane never made it to it's final destination thanks to the brave actions of the men and women on that plane.

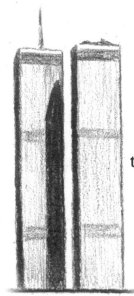

Unfortunately when the south tower fell, the church crumbled under the massive intensity of the collapsing towers. No one was in the church when it collapsed.

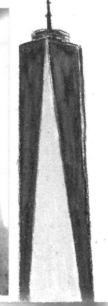

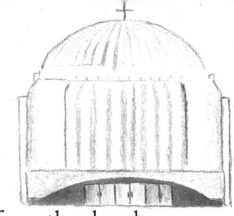

Not much was found from the church.

All that was found was an icon, a bible, pages from a liturgical book, and wax candles.

After 15 years St. Nicholas is finally being rebuilt in the same space as the 9/11 memorial and museum. It will be the only religious building on the site.

The St. Nicholas National Shrine will be open to all denominations and faiths as a place to grieve and find peace. The church will also function as a traditional Greek Orthodox Church and will serve Sunday services, funerals, weddings, baptisms, etc.

The architect for the St. Nicholas National Shrine is Santiago Calatrava.

When the church is complete, it will produce a slight glow at night reminding people that even in the darkest of places there is light and that even in despair, there is hope.

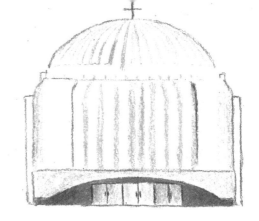

On September 11, 2001, many lives were lost and for a long time there did not seem to be much hope. We will never forget the brave men and women who died that day. Now, through the rebuilding of St. Nicholas Church, there is hope for a better future, one with peace and light. The new St. Nicholas, just as the original, will be a light in the shadow.

Special thank you to Andrew Veniopoulos at the Greek Orthodox Archdiocese of America for answering all of my questions about St. Nicholas.

To find out more information about St. Nicholas National Shrine please go to https://www.stnicholaswtc.org

For more information about the events of September 11, 2001, please visit http://www.911memorial.org/museum

Image Credits
PAGE #38-40. Courtesy Greek Orthodox Archdiocese of America

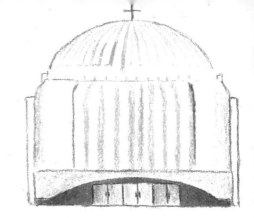

AuthorHouse™
1663 Liberty Drive
Bloomington, IN 47403
www.authorhouse.com
Phone: 1 (800) 839-8640

Published by AuthorHouse 01/16/2017

ISBN: 978-1-5246-5438-2 (sc)
ISBN: 978-1-5246-5437-5 (e)
ISBN: 978-1-5246-5436-8 (hc)

Print information available on the last page.

This book is printed on acid-free paper.

author**HOUSE**®

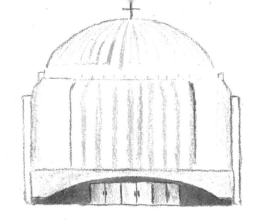

About the Book

Meet Anastasia, a very special candle. Anastasia, along with St. Nicholas Greek Orthodox Church became a symbol of hope and light after the tragic events of September 11, 2001. Anastasia's journey begins in the year 1919, as she travels to New York City and finds a home in the church. She shares with the reader, daily events and special moments she and her family become a part of over the years. Through the beautifully illustrated pages, her courageous journey comes to life. The book tells her story through the events of September 11, 2001 up until the historic rebuild of The St. Nicholas National Shrine. Anastasia holds hope for a brighter future not only for her home in New York City, but for the world.

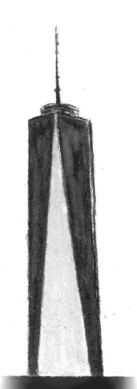

CPSIA information can be obtained
at www.ICGtesting.com
Printed in the USA
BVHW02s1541101018
529801BV00014B/169/P